Copyright © 2023 by VH Nicolson

Published by: Kristina Fair Publishing Ltd

This book is a work of fiction. Characters, names, organizations, places, events and incidents are the product of the author's imagination and any resemblance to actual person, living or dead, is entirely coincidental.

Editing by Sarah Baker, The Word Emporium.

Cover image: © Shutterstock

AUTHOR'S NOTES

Please note this book comes with a content warning. This book is intended for over 18s. My books all come with the guarantee of a happily ever after but sometimes the journey to get there can be a hard fought one. The main focus of my books is love, romance and happiness. Please keep that in mind. Also there is lots of humor too. However, just in case you aren't sure, and if you are a sensitive reader then please proceed with caution, here's a content warning list.

Triggers: Accidental death, Abandonment

For Content Warnings & Tropes of All My Books, Please Scan the QR Code Above.

PREFACE

If you've never had the pleasure of visiting Castleview Cove, the quaint seaside town situated on the north east of Scotland, and featured in both my Triple Trouble Series and The Boys of Castleview Cove Series, then let me fill you in...

It's a magical little town where miles of golden beaches outline the town's perimeter. The town may be small, but it attracts droves of tourists all year round.

Cozy coffee and cupcake shops, Championship golf courses, award-winning ice cream parlors, busy harbors, and miles of pier to amble along are a few of the Castleview Cove must-dos.

Thirteenth Century buildings litter the town, and of course, there's the castle that keeps a watchful eye over everyone; it's central to everything.

Breathtaking, romantic, and comforting, Castleview Cove will feel like you're cozied up by the fire, with a hot cup of cocoa and snuggled up with your best friend for a good gossip; which there is plenty of in the fictional town of Castleview.

It's a tiny place filled with cobbled streets, where everyone knows everyone, and when there's a new business in town, or well, a restaurant, then of course there must be a story behind it...

CHAPTER 1

HOLLY - THREE WEEKS BEFORE CHRISTMAS

Preparing myself for what's about to happen, the wooden stairs I'm sitting on creak underneath me as I lengthen my spine and push my shoulders back, willing false confidence to hide how utterly wrecked I feel.

Ironically, the faint sound of my favorite Christmas song, 'Last Christmas' by Wham! melodically floats from the radio in my kitchen into the hallway.

This is Travis' first... and last Christmas with me.

"Hey, Holly." Travis closes my front door, and a faint gust of unwelcome frosty air enters my snug home, hitting my shins, and causing me to shiver.

I clench my fingers together on my lap and throw him the sweetest smile I can muster. "Hi."

"What's this?" He points to the black trash bags piled up on the wooden floor.

"Your stuff." I grin wider, continuing to stare at him, which must make me look like a homicidal maniac.

"What?" He begins removing his thick woolen overcoat.

Stopping him in his tracks, I firmly say, "Keep your coat on. You won't be staying."

"Sugar?" Confusion runs deep along the wrinkles of his forehead.

"Don't. Call. Me. *Sugar*," I mutter. My clenched jaw wants to roar out the words... scream them out loud, and finally tell him that I hate his pet name for me, but I don't. I refuse to let him see the humiliation I feel deep in my bones.

I've hated that stupid name since the first time he called me it when we started dating six months ago.

Six months. What a waste.

Pushing his hands into the pockets of his coat, Travis continues to look at me like I've grown a set of reindeer antlers.

I've got to hand it to him—the bemused look he's giving me is the exact same look that's lined his face for the past two months. The one plastered on his face every time I've questioned him about where he's been when he doesn't come home for dinner, or why he's been working until midnight, or why, suddenly, his manager sends him away on overnight 'business trips' when he works in a call center for an insurance company, that requires no travel. Or overtime. Ever.

He scoffs nervously, stepping backward. It's almost as if he knows I know.

Beads of sweat shimmer across his forehead and I'm positive it's not the heat of my cozy house that's causing him to sweat as much as he is.

"I-I don't understand," he stutters lowly.

I wave my hand over the bags as if I'm a magician's assistant. "All of your belongings." I pause before delivering my killer blow. "I'm kicking you out. It's amazing how much shit you've accumulated, considering you don't officially live here." He's been wedging his way in day by day, it would seem, and I never even noticed.

"What?" he gasps, as if he wasn't expecting my reaction. "Why?"

"Do you *really* need me to explain?" I ask, my tone flat.

"You can't kick me out." Looking panicked, he arcs his neck, twisting it side to side, then runs his finger inside the collar of his white dress shirt.

"I can. I never asked you to move in. This is my house. My rules. Now pick up your crap and get out." My heart is punching against my chest. I can feel it in my throat, making me feel like my whole body is vibrating, but I force myself to hide how betrayed I feel.

Travis runs his hand down his tie, then lets out a sigh. "What's up, Sugar? Is it that time of the month?"

My blood boils. He's got some nerve trying to pull that line on me. He has a way of redirecting our problems back onto me. Normally, his verbal backflips land. Not tonight, they won't. I won't let them. Not anymore.

"Ha-ha. Good one. Nice try on the deflection," I laugh mockingly, pulling myself to my feet. "You have five minutes to leave."

His jaw drops. "You're actually being serious?" he questions, his tone sounding strangled.

"Deadly." I rest one hand between the strands of twinkling fairy lights I've threaded around the stair handrail and pop a hip. "Leave your keys on the side." I stare him down, pointing in the direction of the console table.

I eye my freshly manicured red glittery nails, admiring them as if I don't have a care in the world. It's all a front. In reality, my joy has been stolen. He took it. My manicure may be shiny and sparkly; however, I'm lacking luster, and quite frankly, in comparison to the girl Travis has apparently been cheating on me with, I'm *dull*.

From the texts they have been sharing that I've read, I don't sound as adventurous as *Tiffany*. I've never been interested in swimming with sharks or cliffside camping. It sounds hideous. Horrifically dangerous and cold.

Travis sweetens his tone, running his fingers through his hair again as he takes a few steps toward me. "Sugar. Baby. At least tell me what I've done wrong, so we can talk about this."

"Okay," I sigh. "Let's chat and get this over with." I reach down to pick up his computer tablet I've been waiting to use as evidence.

Not protected by a password, I swipe it open. The asshole clearly thinks I'm not clever enough to look at it. "Where shall we start?" I begin reading out the first text that grabs my attention. "Ah, this will do... *Can't wait to see you later baby, I've been thinking about you all day*." I sweeten up my voice, making it sound flirty.

I look up.

Travis' skin color turns ashen. "Don't do this," he begs.

Ignoring him, I read out text after text between the two of them.

Does she suspect anything?

When will your husband be home?

Meet me in the server room, big boy.

I'll leave her soon. Just give me some more time.

Just tell her you are going away on business.

And the one that hurt the most... **I can't wait to put a ring on your finger.**

What money is he buying a ring with? Mine? My

inheritance?

I know for a fact Travis doesn't have any money of his own. He's flat broke. He has student loans up to his ball sack and credit card bills galore, which is why he still stays with his mother... or me, it would now appear.

I click my tongue. "How were you planning on paying for a ring exactly? And she's married, right? This Tiffany girl? So how is marrying her even possible?" I place the tablet down on the table. "She sounds like a stand-up gal. A real girl's girl." I hate cheaters. "And you'll have to wait until she gets a divorce if you want to marry her. Or perhaps she's a bigamist, or is she into polyamorous relationships? Does her husband want that, too? Maybe we should ask him. What's his name again?" I look down at the screen that's still glowing bright with the evidence of his lies, knowing exactly what Tiffany's husband's name is. "Oh, yeah, Simon." I look up, anger blazing in my eyes. "Your boss."

Panic flares across his face and he pulls his handkerchief from his pocket to dab his sweaty brow, before waving it like a white flag in mock surrender. "Please don't tell him. She meant nothing to me, I swear. I was never going to leave you. I love you. You are my everything." His tone is sickly sweet, as if his words will make me forgive him.

"Can you love two people?" I pick up the tablet and flip the screen to show him, pointing at the words, **I love you,** that he sent to her. Words he's probably whispered in her ear as he fucked her in their rendezvous spot in the server room.

The idea of them together makes me want to vomit. But I don't, even though the sour bile bubbling in my throat is giving me heartburn.

My only saving grace is that he hasn't touched me in months. Sex became just a distant memory in our relationship. And one I was happy to live without.

"Holly, please believe me." His voice is high now, almost desperate.

I toss the tablet on top of the sacks stuffed with his belongings, making them rustle and hiss under the falling weight of the device. Sitting in the sea of black, it glares brightly, mocking me.

"I believe those messages. They are there in black and white. You can't expect me to believe a word that comes out of your mouth." I let out a hollow laugh. "You must think I'm naïve and stupid. But here's where you are wrong." I pause, making sure I articulate my feelings as best I can. "Your own stupidity caught you out. Linking your phone to your tablet proves to me *you're* the dumb one. I've read every one of those messages and I know for a fact she is never leaving her husband. I know Tiffany better than you do. I know the size of the house her and Simon live in. I know she was his secretary before they were even a thing. How many other guys do you think she's been with in your office? Made the same promises to?" I tap my finger on my bottom lip as if thinking. "Oh, I also know she likes the finer things in life. The parties, five-star holidays. Four, sometimes, five times a year. You're gullible if you believe she is ever leaving him for you. You have no house to offer her, no savings, no car, no money. Nothing."

"I have a car." He spits venom my way.

"Eh, no." I hold my pointer finger up in the air. "I bought you that car. It's in my name so you can leave those keys on the side, too." I swing my finger in the direction of the wooden console table again. The one that's been there since I was a little girl.

"You can't do this." His voice getting louder each time he speaks.

"Do what?"

"Throw me out," He replies, his loud voice vibrating off the walls.

"That's where you're mistaken. I've never asked you to move in here. However, you have been living under my roof, rent free, for months. You weaseled your way in here. You've never even offered to pay any of the bills or for groceries. You expect everything and give nothing in return."

The realization of how much he's taken me for granted begins to dawn on me, making me even angrier and more desperate to get this man out of my house.

"Oh, come on, Holly." He flings his hands out to the side, motioning to the space we are standing in. "It's not like you can't afford it. You inherited this house and a shit ton of money. You have hundreds of thousands of pounds in the bank, and I know for a fact you've barely touched any of it."

Not that it's any of his business, but that money is for opening a second restaurant. My first, Luminescence, has been so successful in Castleview Cove, I have plans to open one in Bayview, the next village over, too.

I throw my head back and let out a sarcastic chuckle. "The most laughable part of all this is that you seriously thought you would get your hands on my money." To buy Tiffany a ring. How ironic; Tiffany won't get a ring from Tiffany the jewelers. It's more likely to be a plastic ring from a Christmas cracker.

Anger flies through my blood, making it boil like lava, but I keep my voice steady. "You are a low-life piece of shit and not worthy of my time."

He steps forward, but I stand firm and point in the

direction of the front door. "I'm not saying this again. Pick up your stuff and leave."

"But it's only three weeks until Christmas. Where am I going to go?"

"Back to your mother's house," I say sweetly. "Your home. You know, where you are *supposed* to live."

He sighs. "I can't move back in with my mom. She's converted my old bedroom into her sewing room."

Wow, that was quick. She clearly wants him out of her house, too. I mean, after all, he is thirty-two years old. A grown man who acts like a boy.

I should have paid attention to the red flags.

"Call someone who cares. Because I don't."

Swiveling around on the balls of my feet, I skip up the stairs and call back over my shoulder, "You have five minutes. Tick, tock. Oh, and have a lovely Christmas, Travis," I feign joyfulness.

I start getting changed to distract myself from the rustling, scuffling sounds, and Travis' mutterings about how *I'm selfish... I don't deserve him... I'm the Grinch... Christmas would be crap with me anyway... no Christmas tree up... blah, blah, blah,* I quickly remove my black shift dress and high-heeled black patent shoes then slip into a clean pant suit.

Throwing my cheating boyfriend out onto the street was the last thing I planned to do when I came home tonight between split shifts, especially after the day, well month, I've had. But then I found his computer tablet, confirming everything I've suspected for weeks.

And as I hear the door click shut and silence descend on the house, I realize here I am, alone at Christmas... again.

CHAPTER 2

HOLLY - FOUR DAYS BEFORE CHRISTMAS

My feet are killing me. I give my toes a wiggle in my flat pumps, trying to relieve the pain, as I have another shift to cover at the restaurant tonight.

Again.

I'm tired. Exhausted, in fact. I am counting down the days until I can have Christmas and Boxing Day off in four days.

Even though I'll be spending it alone.

My heart sinks another two inches deeper into the cavity of my chest.

Today is yet another hectic day at the restaurant. Almost every member of my staff has fallen ill with the stomach flu virus that's doing the rounds and I'm praying—in fact, my only wish to Santa is for a full healthy team of staff in the New Year, as I have a fully booked restaurant for the next six months.

When I finally ticked a goal off my list and used some of my inheritance money to open a restaurant this year, I honestly didn't realize how hard it was going to be. From

9

employing staff, designing logos for the restaurant, purchasing staff uniforms, sourcing food suppliers, retaining and motivating staff, organizing contractors, meetings with accountants, and endless menu changes... Being a restaurant manager for someone else's business was easy, but now that I'm in charge of my own restaurant, I realize how unprepared I am.

Regardless, I love it and it makes me jump out of bed every morning, knowing that I am doing what I always dreamed of. I've never been so motivated.

But the motivation does nothing for my exhaustion. Yet again today, three members of staff called in sick, and therefore, me and my restaurant manager waitressed a fully booked lunch shift. My feet continue to throb at the memory.

As a restaurant owner, I've done more waitressing this last month than actual management.

"Why is this not working?" I tap my finger furiously against the restaurant till touchscreen, praying my repetitive poking will somehow magically turn it back on.

"Well, that's not going to help, is it?" Jenna, my restaurant manager, grabs my wrist to stop me, then lowers it to my side. "Calm. Your. Shit, Holly."

Out of character and most unexpectedly, I burst into tears, staring at the blackened screen.

"Hey, hey. C'mon," Jenna coos as she gently hooks her arm around my shoulder. She pulls me in close to her side and lays her head on my other shoulder.

"I know it's been a tough few weeks."

"Months," I mumble.

"Okay, months. It could be worse," she sighs. "We could be Castle Cones Ice Cream Parlor with no electricity, freezers full of ice cream, dozens of Baked Alaska orders to fulfill for Christmas orders, but forced to shut up shop and write off stock, losing lots of money in the process."

She's right, it could be so much worse.

Jenna continues, "It's only a computer, Holly. People will still turn up for their tables. We have food, a fully booked restaurant. Two of the kitchen staff are helping to wait tables tonight, plus me and you. We can do this."

"But we don't know what time people are coming and how many people are on each table," I interject, swiping the droplets of sadness off my chin, then splay my fingers in the direction of the till, splashing my salty tears on the lifeless screen.

"Can we not have one week… just one week… that's all I am asking for, where we don't have any hiccups?"

She gives me a few moments to calm down and regain my composure before she speaks again.

"You good?" she asks.

I round my shoulders and straighten my spine, trying to pretend I'm better than I feel. "I'm fine." I clear my throat, run my forefingers under my eyes lightly, being careful not to smudge my mascara, then smooth my figure-hugging red dress across my hips. Blowing out a breath, I say, "I'm perfectly fine." *I can do this.*

"You'll never get laid with red puffy cheeks and a face looking like a slapped ass." She nudges my shoulder, making me laugh. "It's Christmas. No more tears. Also, for selfish reasons, I need to make sure you are sparkly and bright over the holidays. No more sadness, okay?"

"Okay," I say with fake enthusiasm, trying to summon at least a slither of joy.

I haven't told her, or anyone, that I'm spending Christmas alone.

I'm grateful I have Jenna in my life. She really is an

angel. "I'll call the company. Get them to come out again to get to the root of the problem," she announces as she picks up the telephone and dials the help desk number stuck to the side of the till. "It's a brand-new system. It shouldn't just switch itself off and not come back on."

Twisting my neck to look at her, I mouth, *thank you.*

With her ear pressed against the phone, she gives me a reassuring wink. "Any excuse to get the IT hottie back here. I'm down with that and I'm sure he will be, too. He couldn't take his eyes off you last week when he was here. What was his name again?"

"I don't remember." I lie, knowing damn fine what his name is.

Jenna rests her hip against the reception desk and frowns, as if deep in thought. "Gar, George? Began with a G. Ga... Ga... Gabe... that was it." Her eyebrows playfully wiggle up and down.

Yup, that was it. Everything about him was kind of difficult to forget.

"Gabe was a babe." She giggles.

He really was a babe. Like a living, breathing Clark Kent. Big muscles, geek chic, thick rimmed, black glasses, dark wavy hair, hazel eyes, broad, tall. Did I list big? Huge, in fact. Huge and gorgeous.

Jenna casts her gaze around the restaurant, assessing our situation. "We'll set all the tables up, and we can reshuffle if we need to as diners arrive. We have two hours before we open for the evening. Plenty of time to sort this." She points at the screen.

"Oh..." She holds her pointer finger in the air as the person on the other end answers her call. "Hi, this is Jenna from Luminescence."

I listen to her arrange an emergency technician visit with a sigh of relief.

Picking up the electric blue colored menus I walk into the main body of the restaurant to begin setting the tables for the evening.

Feeling every heavy footstep as I trudge around the restaurant, I don't feel festive. Not even in the slightest.

I do a mental countdown.

Four days until Christmas.

Three Christmas presents bought; one each for my best friend Lucy, her husband Alan, and their daughter, my goddaughter, Izzy. They've already been wrapped and delivered since they are off to spend the holidays with Alan's parents in Glasgow.

Two bottles of wine in the fridge, ready for me to celebrate the holidays.

And one little present from Lucy, Alan, and Izzy sitting, waiting to be opened on top of my fireplace in my living room.

I don't have a Christmas tree to put it under as I haven't put one up this year.

We have decorations and a tree up in the restaurant, though. That counts, right? I mean, this is *my* business, my second home, so to speak.

I take a moment to admire my beautiful restaurant. True to its name, Luminescence, it lights me up. Every inch of it. Every decision made, every color used, the table positions, fabric choices, menu options, the neon blue lighting... I created it all, and it makes my heart sing.

The restaurant was created to allow diners to taste exquisite foods in multi-sensory ways. We design illusion food, bursting with flavor. From savory pâtés made to look like fruit to ice cream deserts that look like bacon and eggs. I sourced the best kitchen chemistry chefs from across the country and together we created culinary creations that are talked about for miles around.

It's elite dining at its finest.

I invested almost all my inheritance from my mother and father into my dream and I have plans to open a sister restaurant with what my grandmother left me, too.

That's if I can manage it. I already feel stressed and wrung out and we've only been open six months. I am trusting that the craziness settles down and we have a glitch-free week soon.

The New Year perhaps?

I tilt my head back and look up through the glass ceiling of the orangery, at the darkening inky sky above.

If only my folks and grandmother could see what I've created.

"This is for you guys," I whisper. I hope they are looking down on me and are proud of what I've achieved.

Jenna shouts across to me, "They are sending a technician. They'll be here in ten minutes."

My gaze fixes on the North Star, as I let out a grateful sigh. "That's fast," I call back.

"There was one in the area. We timed that well." She scuffles about behind me.

I keep my eyes trained on the stars. "Thank you," I reply, not knowing if I'm thanking Jenna for organizing a technician or my guardian angels for looking out for me.

I think both.

CHAPTER 3

Holly

I'm standing on the other side of our reservations desk. "Who invented this stupid system, anyway?" I ask Gabe, the babe, er, I mean, Gabe, just Gabe. *Get it together, sister.*

Feeling flustered as deep brown eyes stare at me from across the top of black-rimmed glasses. "That would be me." One of his eyebrows shoots up in amusement.

"Oh." *Dammit. Stop insulting him, Holly.*

I can't take my eyes off him. He's even more gorgeous than I remember; book smart and super sexy.

"I'm sorry," I whisper. "It's good. It really is... when it works. That's why I picked this piece of software. You must be super clever if you created it." I chew on my bottom lip nervously.

With hooded eyes, he stares at me, lingering on my mouth for a beat before they drop down my body, to the deep *V* neckline of my red dress, and back up again, feeling like he's mentally undressing me. The thick veins of his neck protrude from his skin as he clenches his square, muscular jaw.

It's so sharp, you could slice your tongue on it.

I don't care, I'd still like to lick it.

A peculiar feeling deep in my core ignites as I continue to stare back.

Gabe finally breaks the magic spell that felt like it was momentarily cast between us when he dips his head and fixes his attention back on the screen. I let out a frustrated breath, mad at myself for insulting him and also a little annoyed that he's not looking at me anymore.

My tummy does a flippy thing every time his eyes are on me, something I have yet to make sense of, as it's never happened with anyone before. But it's something I want to happen again and again because it means he's looking at me and I like how it makes me feel.

Gabe is nice, super-hot and I'm a female, so I can appreciate that he's, well, all man. He smells delicious—like frankincense and sin, all rolled into one. Every time he moves, his spicy scent assaults my nose and I swear, it makes all the hairs on my body stand to his attention. But I haven't had sex in months, so maybe my body is overreacting because I'm feeling desperate.

Maybe that's what's going on here because I can't explain my body's reaction to him. It's... different, new, exciting. Overwhelming.

I wonder what sex would be like with Gabe, the babe. To feel my hands running through his wavy, dark, glossy locks, as he licked my neck and asked me to come for him like a good girl. Imagining him asking me if I've been naughty or nice this year.

Bad. Very bad, Gabe.

"I beg your pardon, Holly?"

I snap out of my fantasy when he says my name.

With amusement written all over his face, he flashes me a megawatt smile.

"Mmmm?" A warm flush cascades across my skin.

"You said you've been bad, very bad. Have you? Are you on the naughty list this year, Angel?"

Angel?

"Ha." Nervous laughter escapes my throat when I realize I must have spoken my wayward thoughts. I point at him backing away from the desk before he sues me for sexual harassment as well as insulting his software programme. "I'll leave you to... you know." I do some sort of weird fake gun gesture with my pointer fingers. "Get on with the techy whizzy stuff."

Jesus Christ, Holly, you're a professional businesswoman. Pull yourself together.

I swivel around too fast on the balls of my feet, trip over and let out a high-pitched yelp as I fall against one of the black dining tables, making the silverware jingle on the tabletop.

Strong hands loop around my waist, surrounding me in a haze of Gabe's scent. "I got you." He rights my stance, spinning me around slowly in his warm, broad arms.

"Thank you," I whisper as I lean into his hold. I don't want him to let me go.

He tenderly tucks a strand of my dark hair behind my ear. "Has anyone ever told you how beautiful you are, Holly?"

Not in a very long time, and Jenna doesn't count.

"Can I take you out for dinner one night?" His remaining hand presses harder into the small of my back as he runs his thumb up and down the base of my spine.

I swallow hard, realizing he's asking me on a date. "I

own a restaurant." *What a stupid thing to say. I love eating out... I'd love him to eat me out.*

"The theater then?"

"Not a fan of musicals. Why can't they speak to each other instead of singing it?"

He chuckles. "Ice skating?"

I freeze. There is no way I could revisit that hideous memory. "I can't, I..."

"Okay." He nods, looking rejected. "I can take the hint, Angel." He moves his mouth to the shell of my ear. "Such a pity. I would have loved to find out whether you've been a good or a bad girl this year."

He leans back and I'm so embarrassed and flustered by him that I can't look him in the eye.

And then he's gone, leaving his heady fragrance clinging to the fabric of my dress.

Shit, I should have said yes.

The words of my grandma ring in my ears. *'Don't let your past dictate your future.'*

Before I can change my mind and beg him to take me out, I dash through the restaurant, pushing the swing doors of the kitchen open so hard it ricochets off the wall. I don't look back and head straight out of the delivery entrance into the small staff car park behind the restaurant.

Sucking the fresh chilly air deep into my lungs, my heated breath evaporates into the frosty night in huge puffs of smoke-like clouds.

"You alright?" Jenna appears outside in an instant.

"He wanted to take me ice skating," I say quietly.

She throws her thumb back over her shoulder in the direction of the restaurant. "How was he to know?"

Nodding in agreement at my stupidity, I let out a small laugh. Of course, he wouldn't know. He's not from

Castleview Cove. I would remember him if he was and Castleview is so small that everyone knows everyone. Gabe is someone I don't know, but I'd like to.

"I should have said yes. Isn't that what my therapists told me to do? Face your fear. Feel the fear and do it, regardless." I throw my hands to the sky, feeling like an idiot. "I should have said yes, shouldn't I?"

"You can still say yes," Jenna reminds me as she hugs her arms around herself in a feeble attempt to protect herself from the freezing temperature.

The weatherman on the radio this morning said we are getting snow tomorrow. Not usually a gambler, I'm now wishing I had put a bet on having a white Christmas. The odds are high that we are most definitely getting one in Castleview Cove this year.

A gust of icy air makes me shudder. "We should go back inside. It's bloody freezing now the sun has set. However, freezing temps or not, I think I'll wait here until Gabe leaves. He'll think I've lost the plot."

I already feel like I've lost control. This restaurant has taken over my life. I look back through the fire exit door of the kitchen that Jenna is holding open, and standing in the doorway is a broad shouldered, incredibly tall, Gabe-shaped silhouette.

He moves out into the car park, the gravel crunching under his feet with every confident step in my direction.

"Sorry for eavesdropping, but I would never think you've lost the plot. I think you're an incredibly capable, talented businesswoman, who has a fully booked out restaurant for the next six months, and a waiting list longer than Santa's naughty or nice list." He anchors his attention on me as he walks closer. "I know this because your software is fixed. You had a Christmas grinch in there

19

causing chaos in the system. A glitch. But he's gone. All sorted."

Relief threads through my tight muscles, the knots in my shoulders sagging because he not only fixed my booking software, he fixed everything. That software manages the entire restaurant; reservations, staff payroll, rosters, stock... everything.

That's one less headache. I'll be able to pay my staff correctly and I'll have happy suppliers and customers.

While I think about how this one man has single handily saved Christmas, my heart flutters at the lovely things he said about me. *Incredibly capable, talented.* Me?

"Thank you." A soft smile curves my lips. "I'm very grateful."

"So am I," Jenna interjects. I almost forgot she was here. "I'll go set the tables up correctly since we're no longer winging it tonight," Jenna announces, heading back through the open door, leaving me standing with Gabe. Alone.

He removes his glasses, tucking them into the back pocket of his trousers, giving me a better view of his handsome features.

"Everyone is talking about your illusion food and the vibe you've created here." Gabe widens his stance, pushing his hands into the pockets of his navy dress trousers.

I can't help but notice the outline of his thick length beneath the fabric, and it's not even hard; his pants are working overtime to conceal it.

"It's such a cool concept," he adds. "You've created a whole new dining experience. An exclusive dining package."

I want to unwrap his package.

God, I need to get laid.

It's been too long and my vibrating purple friend is no

longer doing it for me. I need connection, touch, to feel taken care of, to feel loved.

I have to fight hard to stem the tears that threaten to fall when I think about how long it's been since I have felt loved. It's been a very long time.

Everyone I've ever loved, or that has ever loved me, has gone. I lost them all.

I've never felt so alone... so devastatingly lonely.

I thought opening the restaurant would help fill the empty void I've been feeling, but it hasn't. All it's done is keep me busy. It's been a good distraction. It's helped me fill the hours in the day, but it doesn't make up for how alone I feel.

I think about why I wanted to start up the restaurant in the first place. I wanted to do it for *them*; my parents.

I open my mouth and let my words spill out into the cold night air. "It's been a dream of mine since I was a little girl. I loved cooking, baking, and creating unusual foods with my mom. She was a chef. A brilliant one. She always spoke about opening a restaurant. My dad would manage it, she would cook and I would be the best hostess in the world she said." I chuckle at the fond memory. She always used to say that my dad was too grumpy to greet people; his deep gruff voice and frank manner would scare people away. Maybe his outward demeanor would have, but he was the biggest, gentlest, loving man I've ever known. He loved my mom, and me, unconditionally.

"You said *was*? Did she not open one?" A deep *V* forms in the middle of his forehead.

"She passed away. They both did." I don't elaborate, it's too painful.

"I'm so sorry, Holly." I've only met Gabe a handful of times, but I know the sound of sincerity when I hear it.

"It was a long time ago." But I've never completely gotten over it and very rarely talk about what happened. Like now, I don't want to talk about any of it. Tears prick at my eyes as my long-buried emotions fight to be heard. "We should go back in." My voice cracks as I point to the illuminated doorway, begging me to enter the warmth it holds within.

I brush past Gabe, desperate to end this conversation, but he gently catches the top of my upper arm, holding me firmly, instantly stopping me in my tracks. With a swift movement, I'm pulled into his arms and enveloped in the most unexpected warm embrace as he wraps his bulging biceps around me.

What is this stranger doing? Why is he hugging me?

In an attempt to stop his moment of insanity, I grab onto his waist to push him away, but he ignores it, pulling me into his strong frame, holding me tighter.

"What... what are you doing?" I try pulling back again, but he holds me against his chest. I can't deny how delicious he smells, how good his arms feel around me, and how much I would like to stay wrapped in his arms... forever.

I feel safe, content, *his.*

Aw Christmas crackers... where did that come from?

"I want to make you feel better," he whispers. "You always look so sad. I want to take all your pain away," he tells me, resting his chin on the top of my head, as if we've done this a million times before. "When was the last time you had a day off, Holly?"

My body tenses. I wonder if it's obvious to everyone how much I am struggling to keep on top of everything. And if I'm wearing my grief like a badge of honor.

"Relax, Angel," he murmurs, as if he can read my mind. "To everyone else, you look as if you're bossing it. Holding everything together perfectly. But I can see all the secrets you hide behind those beautiful green eyes."

My heart hammers as inquisitive fingers slide from my waist, up my back, threading themselves into my hairline before clasping the back of my head with his bear sized hands as he presses my face into his solid chest.

As if someone popped me with a pin, I feel boneless; my body deflating, as he caresses me, cocooning me in his thick arms.

"Why are you doing this?"

"I feel your pain, your exhaustion. I can feel the vibration of the constant bustle in your head. You need a day off."

"I'll get one on Christmas and Boxing Day." I mumble against the soft baby blue of his dress shirt, losing myself in his heady frankincense scent. He smells like what I imagine Christmas joy would smell like. "You smell nice."

His lips brush against my neck as he nuzzles in. "Never mind how *I* smell... I'm wondering how *you* taste." I gasp when his smooth lips kiss behind my ear, sending rivulets of goosebumps exploding up and down my spine.

The tip of his tongue against my skin pulls a deep moan from his throat.

I tilt my head to the side, giving him permission to kiss me again. And as he does, my fingers move, burying themselves into the bottom of his wavy locks.

Suddenly I long for him to bite me, mark me, brand me as his.

As if sensing my thoughts, he nips at my skin, licks, then kisses my neck; harder this time.

"Kiss me." I moan, my request sends a billow of white clouds into the air as warm hits cold.

His eyes lock with mine as if he's looking deep into my

soul, then he cups my face. "I've wanted to kiss you since the first day we met. Only you had a boyfriend then."

I pull my brows together. "How did you know that?"

"Jenna told me. She also told me that you broke up with him."

"She's got a big mouth." I say, secretly pleased she told him. "He cheated on me." I shouldn't have over shared. I still feel the mortification of my discovery. Jenna keeps telling me it wasn't my fault, but it feels like it was.

"He was a fool."

"I got busy. Distracted. I didn't pay him enough attention."

"That's no excuse."

He's right, it's not.

"You're really beautiful, Angel." His mouth pulls to the side. "Do you really want me to kiss you? If so, I want to hear you say those words again."

My bold eyes search his for a beat then I shamelessly say, "Kiss me. I want you."

"You do?" His gaze drops to my lips.

"I do," I confess.

Bowing his head, his lips hover over mine briefly, before his mouth captures mine. Fireworks explode as our lips touch for the first time, mine parting in a silent groan. Pushing his tongue inside, he kisses me like his life depends on it. As if he wants to hold on to my heart and never let go.

I might not let him.

Much taller than me, I rise on my tiptoes to offer him more of myself. To go deeper, to connect us, to devour him.

This feels so right, so good, so perfect. It's so good that I'm sure I can hear choirs of angels singing Christmas carols somewhere in the distance.

Gabe wraps my long dark hair around his fist and

deepens our kiss, while the other circles my waist. He lets out a growl-like noise when his now hard length rubs against my hip.

I tighten my grip on the strands of his hair, pushing his scruff covered face into mine. He doesn't seem to care as I squash our noses together, making us both struggle for breath. In a trance-like spin, I feel the most incredible pleasure I've ever experienced... from just his kiss. A life changing, transformational kiss.

Gabe pulls back breathlessly and says, "You taste like magic." Then he kisses across my jaw. "So. Fucking. Beautiful." Down my neck. "Say yes." He licks, then nips my decolletage.

"To what?" I groan.

"A date." He lifts his head, his mouth finding mine, and our desperate tongues frantically twist together again.

"I can do one better," I mutter against his lips, throwing caution to the winter wind.

"Oh, really?" he replies, biting down gently on my bottom lip, sparking a flutter of butterflies in my stomach.

"Mmmmm." I can't speak. I don't want to stop kissing him as I melt under the heat of his mouth. I'm so turned on, the spark between my thighs, now an electric ball of fire and a heavy ache of need.

I need him inside me, now.

His thumb brushes my jawline as he slows the pace of our hectic encounter, leaning out of our kiss, leaving his lips lingering over mine.

Lazily opening my eyes, I find him staring at me, with a wicked grin filling his face.

"Tomorrow night," I say before changing my mind. "It's our staff Christmas party. Everyone is bringing a partner. Except for me. Be my plus one?" Embarrassment washes over me now that I've asked him. *Does it make me sound desperate?*

I bounce my eyes back and forth between his, looking for his pity, but it never appears.

"I'll happily be your plus one anytime, Angel." Between his thumb tracing the skin across my cheek, and his other hand perfectly placed on the curve of my waist, I wish I could stay here all night.

Wrapping my arms around his neck, I tuck myself under his chin. "Seven o'clock. Tomorrow night at The Sanctuary. We're closing the restaurant so we can all have a night off together."

He gently sways us, as if we're dancing to a slow love song only we can hear.

"Sounds perfect." He pecks a soft kiss to the top of my head. "I have to go. I have another emergency call to make." His words come out in a whisper.

He entwines his fingers with mine as we step out of our warm embrace. It's minus two out, but I don't feel the biting cold anymore, not even a little.

"I'll pick you up tomorrow." He squeezes my hand, then steals a kiss. "Text me your address."

I giggle, feeling like I'm sixteen again, not thirty-five. "I don't have your number."

"Jenna's already programmed it into your phone." His eyes sparkle with amusement at their cleverness.

"I'm password protecting it as soon as you leave."

His lips curl into a beaming grin, making me feel like I'm being warmed in a puddle of sunshine.

"We should go in. You'll catch a cold if you're out here any longer," he says. For the first time in a very long time, I feel warm and fuzzy inside. The same feeling when I drink hot chocolate with marshmallows and whipped cream in front of a roaring fire on a cold day.

It's been scientifically proven that hot chocolate releases serotonin, making you feel happy and comforted. Just one sip and I can't help but smile.

He's the same. One kiss is all it took to free my happiness.

"I'm going to stay here for just a minute longer," I say. "You go. And I'll see you tomorrow?"

He cups my face once more, kissing my forehead before he confirms the time he's picking me up, reassuring me that, without a doubt, he'll see me tomorrow.

He moves slowly, not letting go of my hand until he's far enough away that his hand is forced to slip from mine, making my arm fall to my side.

Walking back toward to the delivery entrance, he keeps grinning before he throws me a cheeky wink. I give him a flirty finger wave in return watching him swivel around and then disappear through the open door.

I grin to myself and look up at the heavens.

"Seriously? You sent me an angel?" I throw my arms out to the side. "An actual freaking angel? Gabriel? Is this your work you three?" I ask the spirits of my parents and grandma. But I already know it was them. I can feel it.

"Thank you," I shout into the bitter night that's now biting at the tip of my nose and fingers.

I'm seeing him tomorrow.

I do a little happy dance to myself in the middle of the car park.

"Oh, sorry." A gruff voice startles me, and I spin in its direction, coming face to face with our head chef, Thomas, who's holding a vat of old cooking oil.

I smooth my hands over my dress, push my shoulders

back, and make a beeline for the door to take me back into the restaurant.

"Evening, Thomas." I give him a curt nod.

"Evening, Holly." I don't miss his smirk.

Stepping into the warmth, a half chuckle, half splutter breaks from my chest.

I have a date. With an angel.

CHAPTER 4

HOLLY - THREE DAYS BEFORE CHRISTMAS

True to his word, Gabe picked me up just before 7 p.m. ...in a limousine. A freaking limo.

Once I was inside, he placed a beautifully wrapped gold and red bowed gift on my lap.

Astonished by his generosity and thoughtfulness, I gasped when the unwrapped box revealed a stunning gold amulet necklace embossed with a holly tree.

As he fixed the chain around my neck, Gabe informed me the holly tree was a sign from the Celtic zodiac and stood for ruler and leadership. He kissed my nape, then carefully fluffed my hair back in place, he whispered in my ear how he thought I was a trailblazer, a warrior. *A true goddess.*

While I expected him to be considerate, caring, and kind—because that was the type of man he appeared to be—what I didn't expect him to be was jaw-droppingly romantic.

I mean, in less than twenty-four hours, the man had

arranged a limo and then sourced and purchased me a meaningful necklace.

How did he do that?

He's the epitome of the perfect gentleman.

Dressed in the finest of tuxedos, as if it was tailor-made for him, which it most likely was, he's caught more than a little attention this evening from the females in the room.

A vast majority of businesses from Castleview Cove are having their staff Christmas parties here tonight at The Sanctuary, the five-star resort on the outskirts of town. But Gabe's eyes are focused solely on me.

We move together, hip to hip, slowly, across the dance floor, swaying in time to the jazz band playing smooth Christmas songs. Festivity has finally seeped into my bones. It's the first time I've felt a glimmer of holiday spirit in years.

If I have the time, I might even put up a Christmas tree.

"You look sensational tonight. You should be draped in red silk, always. It suits you." Dripping with desire, Gabe's voice sends shivers through me, making every nerve ending in my body come alive. I feel him everywhere.

"My friend, Lucy, is a personal stylist. She did my color analysis; working out what colors suit me best. Red is one of them."

"Is that a thing? Color analysis for people and clothes?"

"It sure is." I squeeze his hand playfully. "And people pay her hundreds of pounds for *such a thing.*"

"Wow. Maybe I should get my colors analyzed." He bites his lower lip as if considering that.

"I think you'd suit the entire rainbow. You look good in everything." I let him know that I see him. All of him. I have since we had the software installed at the restaurant. I found it difficult to concentrate when Gabe ran a three-hour training session with me, Jenna, and Thomas.

He's very distracting. Especially when he speaks with his hands, making the fabric in his shirts struggle not to tear open under the pressure of his huge biceps.

"I don't think you needed your colors analyzed." He spins me three hundred and sixty degrees under his arm.

"No?" My hands land on his chest as I come back to face him.

"I think you'd look better wearing *nothing*." His gaze drops to my lips and stays there for a beat. I'm disappointed he's not wearing his glasses tonight. They make him look super sexy.

"I don't think you need your colors done either." I lick my lips, making his pupils dilate, mesmerized by my glossy red mouth.

"No? Why's that?"

I whisper, "Because I also think you'd look better with nothing on." Then nibble on my bottom lip suggestively.

He moves his mouth to the shell of my ear. "Want to get out of here?"

People started leaving about thirty minutes ago and the band stops playing in ten minutes, so it wouldn't seem rude to my staff if I left now. "My place? It's closer."

Saying a quick goodnight to everyone before I leave, I tell my wonderful team to grab a drink before the bar closes and pass Jenna my credit card. I'm very lucky to have them and I made sure their Christmas bonuses reflected that.

"Let's go." Gabe nuzzles into my neck and then grabs my hand.

I hike my long red dress up at one side to prevent me falling over as we dash across the dance floor toward the exit.

"Holly?" A voice I recognize makes my eyes roll.

Plastering on a fake smile, I turn to face him.

"Hey, Travis," I grit out, grateful that I've managed to avoid him all evening.

Gabe slides his hand around my waist and pulls me into his side, claiming me.

Travis' eyes drop to Gabe's hand, possessively holding onto my hip, then back to my face. "You doing okay? Since we last saw each other?"

Was he expecting me to curl up and die? *Ass wipe*.

"Yeah, I'm great, thanks. You?"

He looks awful. Dark circles under his eyes, hollow cheeks, and his annoying peacock confidence seems to have disappeared.

"I—" His shoulders sag as if defeated. "I'm okay." But his words don't land. He's not okay, he's far from it. I don't care. He made his bed.

"So, Tiffany stayed with her husband then?" I don't need to look over at their table to know she's draped around her husband, where she's been all evening.

"It didn't work out," Travis says, almost inaudibly.

"Aw, that's a shame. You two were really going to do incredible things together. Like cliffside camping and swimming with sharks. Never mind, huh?"

"Look, Holly, can we—"

"Nope. We can never anything." I hold my hand up to stop him from speaking. "Oh gosh, forgive me. Where are my manners? Travis, this is Gabe." Leaning in closer to him, I curl my hand around the top of his arm. *Wow, is that taut?* "Gabe is my—"

"Future husband," Gabe cuts in.

I pull my lips into my mouth to stop myself from laughing at his absurdity and look up at him. *Is that what he wants?* Everything feels like it fades away as if the whole room has disappeared. All I can focus on is his beautiful face and his warm hand cupping my waist.

"It's great chatting and all," he announces to Travis. "But I have a present to unwrap." Gabe's eyes darken as he looks down at me.

I break my gaze with Gabe when I say, "Merry Christmas, Travis."

We don't wait for his reply as we hurry out of the room and into the back of the limo.

CHAPTER 5

HOLLY

Unable to keep our hands off each other once the doors of the limo locked us in, the concealed glass is doing its job by hiding our erotic kisses.

"Straddle me," Gabe instructs, desperation evident in the timber of his voice. With strong arms he pulls me onto his lap, forcing me to wiggle the fine red silk of my dress up my body to accommodate his thick thighs.

My panties now perfectly aligned with his long, hard length, he grunts when my pussy grinds against him, panting into my mouth as he wraps his tongue around mine.

"Gabe," I whimper when he digs his fingertips into my hips, sending waves of slick heat deep in my core. He moves me back and forth, teasing my clit against his covered cock and the fabric of my now wet lace panties.

"I want you," he growls into my mouth when I rock my hips harder, sliding back and forth, chasing my own release. "But I'm not fucking you in a car."

"I don't care." I fumble with the hook and eye of his

black dress pants, tugging at them to move them down his hips.

As if in pain, he groans, considering his options.

"I want you to make me come, Gabe. Right here, right now."

Unable to resist, carelessly, we struggle together, shedding the fabric that's preventing us connecting in the ways I've been imagining all night.

"Jesus fucking Christ, you're going to be trouble." Breaking our kiss, he grits out his words, lifting his hips to help me remove his trousers, taking his boxers with them.

I lift my dress up over my head and drop it somewhere behind me.

Gabe's eyes darken as he takes me in. Gently, he pulls the cup of my red lace bra down, exposing my pebbled nipple. Brushing the pad of his thumb over it, rolling it between his thumb and fingertip, making me cry out with pleasure. "So perfect," he declares before bowing his head and pulls my nipple into his mouth, licking and sucking at my sensitive peak, the bristles from his beard tickling my skin.

I fling my head back, pushing my chest into his face, needing more of him. He flicks my nipple harder with his tongue, then bites down. An electric current of arousal races through my body.

Threading my hands into the back of his hair, I push his face into me, urging him to continue. I want more. I want everything he has to offer.

With his other hand, he slips the soaked red lace of my panties to the side before he slides his cock, glistening with precum, between the lips of my pussy.

Looking down between us, he watches, lips twitching with enjoyment at the place where we connect.

"I'm going to fill with you my cock, Angel."

"Do it now." I move up on my knees, repositioning myself, getting ready to take him. All of him. I gulp at how big he is. "You're so big," I gasp.

"You can take me, Angel. I know you can." He pumps his cock with his fist a few times before lining up the tip to the entrance of my aching pussy. "You're dripping for me."

I lower myself down onto him slowly as he holds the root of his shaft firmly.

"Kiss me." He crashes his lips against mine, distracting me as he pushes his cock into my body at the same time I move down. Rocking together, I ease myself down his huge length, taking him further into my body with every small upward and then downward stroke.

"Oh, God." My eyes roll into the back of my head as he thrusts the final few inches of his shaft up into me.

"Not God, Angel. Gabe. Let me hear my name fall off those pretty little lips of yours."

"Gabe," I cry out as the initial sting of his cock filling me turns into pleasure.

"Say it again," he demands

Louder this time, I shout, not caring that we're in the back of the limo or who might hear us. "Gabe."

He nips at my lips in approval before biting down my neck with gloriously rough kisses.

"I'm going to fill you with my cum," he grunts into my hair.

Startling me back to reality with his words, I gasp. "You're not wearing a condom."

"Shit." He hisses and stops moving, realizing what we're doing. "Do you want to stop? I have a condom in my wallet." He pats his jacket pocket to locate it.

I grab his wrist, stopping him as I say, "I'm clean. Are

you?" Then I confess. "I haven't had sex in a very long time, and I got tested three weeks ago, after, you know..." I don't want to say his name while Gabe is inside of me. "... cheated on me. I'm safe."

"If I told you I haven't had sex for over a year, will you think I'm a loser?" He stares into my eyes. "I'm clean too."

I smile down at him. "I like that I've broken your dry spell."

"You sure have. You are soaked, Angel."

"I have an IUD."

"Well, that's a real fucking shame." He tilts his hips, pushing his cock deep into me, and I can already feel the urge to come.

I moan and frown at the same time, not understanding what he means.

"Because the way you've taken my cock, like such a good girl." He pauses, brushing my hair back over my shoulder. "I want you to be mine. I'm going to marry your fine ass and we're going to fuck every day and have lots of babies."

Oh, my God. Where did this guy come from?

Mild mannered Gabe has turned into a dirty mouthed sex god... and all I can think is I want more of it.

Maybe I should be wondering why his words don't freak me out. Instead they do the opposite. They calm me, knowing that this amazing man, who barely knows me, is confessing, after only a few hours together, that we are going to spend the rest of our lives together. That he *wants* to and wants to start a family. With me. Although my heart wants to believe every word of it, my head is screaming that he's probably only saying it because he wants to have sex with me.

"When you know, you know," he says confidently. "I've

known since the first time I laid eyes on you, Holly. You're *it* for me."

"You're going to ruin me for every other man, aren't you?"

He growls, making his whole chest vibrate. "That's the plan, Angel. There won't be any other men. Just me. Now fuck me and make me *yours*."

Grateful for the privacy glass dividing us from the driver, I press my hand flat against the roof of the limo to give me more leverage.

Tilting my hips, clenching the inner walls of my pussy, I began to move up and down his cock.

I watch pleasure dance over his face as I work out what he likes. Cupping my breasts, he thrusts in deeper, grinding himself against me. He groans when I move faster, the tip of his thick crown teasing my G-spot with every punishing thrust.

"You're so tight. You feel amazing, Angel." The sounds of our bodies moving together fills the small space of the car and I shudder when his thumb finds my clit.

"Gabe," I moan as he circles my sensitive bud, then pinches it. "I'm, I'm gonna—" I stutter my words as my body starts to shake.

"Come," he commands as he pushes up, meeting me thrust for thrust while continuing to swirl his fingertips over my clit.

A blazing hot shock of pleasure burns, radiating into my thighs, and through my wet core. The power of my climax makes my whole body shake, the spasm of my inner walls clench around him, and I let out a high-pitched cry.

"Cover my cock in your cum. That's a good girl." He nuzzles into my neck, his breathing shallow against my skin.

My inner walls flutter around him as the last waves of

my orgasm spill from my body. Twisting slightly, I reach behind me and squeeze his balls. "Oh fuck, Angel. I'm coming." He bucks up into me a few more times as he spills inside of me, groaning as he leans his head back against the leather of the seat.

We pant loudly together as we come down from our high.

"You're perfect," he murmurs. "So, fucking perfect." His cock softens inside of me while my heart feels like it's beating out of my chest, already thinking about round two.

"Stay with me tonight," I whisper in his ear.

"Oh, I intend to. It's going to be a merry *fucking* Christmas, after all." He chuckles at his own joke.

It sure does look like it will be.

CHAPTER 6

Holly - Two Days Before Christmas

The winter sun shines through the gap in the curtains as Gabe lazily slides in and out of me, leisurely enjoying every stroke as he rolls my nipple between his thumb and finger, making my back arch off the bed.

His huge frame, twice my size, envelopes me with his warmth and tenderness.

We fucked all night, in every way possible, and he has made me orgasm so many times, I lost count after the tenth.

"Come for me," he growls against the skin of my neck.

"I can't," I hiss, my sensitive clit throbbing.

"Yes, you can." He pulls out of me, then instructs me to get on all fours.

He slaps my ass when I move onto my knees.

Pulling my hair into a ponytail with one hand, he wraps it around his hand, forcing me to tilt my head back.

Over the course of our evening together, Gabe has flipped from mild-mannered romantic to sex fiend as if not being able to get enough of me.

Having always wanted someone to take control in the bedroom, I like how he makes demands, and how much I love it. It makes me burn for him and makes me so wet, I'm going to need to rehydrate. Stat.

He runs his other hand down my spine. "You should see yourself, Angel. You are fucking beautiful." He digs his fingertips into my hips before laying his body over mine. As if feeling the need to be closer to me, he loops his arm around my waist, pulling my back to his front as he sits back on his hunches, taking me with him.

My thighs straddled on either side of his, Gabe slowly pushes into me from behind. He kisses my shoulder lazily, then up the tilt of my neck to my jaw.

I twist my head, his lips seeking mine, instantly sealing his lips over my mouth. In slow, languid movements, Gabe drives himself into my wet heat and we moan together.

"We're not leaving this bed until you come again for me, Holly," he pants. "Watching you come is the fucking sexiest thing I've ever seen."

Oh God, this man, who I've only known for a few hours, has done everything to make sure that my pleasure is his priority.

I can never imagine doing this with anyone else but him now. He's become my new obsession and someone I know in my gut that I can trust with my whole heart. A pure spirit that I feel connected to in ways I have never experienced before.

He drives himself into me as I rock my hips back and forth. "You are so tight," he groans, his voice sounding even more strained as he fills me completely.

Bucking beneath me, he rubs my clit with his free hand and teases it gently.

There's no rush, but the heat building between us becomes almost unbearable as the head of his cock hits my G-spot over and over.

I let out a low moan I don't recognize as my own; the sounds of our bodies rocking together echoing out into the silence of the room.

"I need to come, Gabe," I whimper.

He flicks my clit, then rubs it softly. Repeating the same motion over and over again until I'm crying his name. Every nerve ending in my body is tuned into his, every cell of my body wants him. I need him in a way that I don't fully understand, but want to explore... again and again until we're both spent.

Overwhelmed by all the sensations he's switched on, he tells me to come for him And I do, experiencing one of strongest orgasms I've ever had. My body shaking with pleasure.

Gabe continues to fuck me through my release as it soars through me. He tenses behind me as he follows me into euphoria, shooting his load.

"Fuck," he groans loudly. His cock continues to jerk inside of me as he spills every last drop.

He plants lazy kisses across my shoulder and neck as I sigh with contentment.

Feelings I can't explain, nor make any sense of flood my heart, making it jackhammer in my chest.

Is this what true love feels like?

Is this what being loved by an angel feels like?

I sure feel like I'm in heaven.

It feels magical.

For the first time since I opened Luminescence, I don't want to go. I want to stay here, with Gabe, snuggled up together in my cozy bed.

I should be getting ready, as I always do on a Sunday, to make my way to open up the restaurant. Although Jenna's on today too, so maybe she could cope by herself for a change?

"Do you have any brothers or sisters?" I ask Gabe, tucking my hand under my cheek as we face each other in my bed.

"Yeah, four sisters and three brothers." His eyes fill with amusement.

"What?" I exclaim. "There are eight of you? Wow, that's a big family."

"We were all fostered," he admits. "Then we were all adopted. My mom and dad are amazing people."

"Eight kids," I whisper to myself.

"When we all get together, it's fun, but very noisy. Especially now that my brothers and sisters have started having kids and there are even more of us. What about you? Any siblings?"

Shaking my head, I say, "Just me."

I can hear his brain working overtime. "What happened to your parents?"

My fingers nervously twitch against my cheek. I clear my throat. "My dad died trying to save my mom."

"Oh, Holly," Gabe whispers, laying his hand over mine where it rests on top of the mattress.

"Her and my dad went for a walk one day, around the lake. The one between Castleview Cove and Bayview."

He nods. knowing the one I am talking about.

"They ventured out onto the frozen water. A few

people saw them, and the police report said they looked happy as they fooled around, laughing and pretending to ice skate in their snow boots. Apparently, my mom fell on the ice, but it wasn't completely frozen." I take a deep breath. "The ice cracked under her weight and she fell under. When she didn't come back up to the surface, Dad jumped in to save her. Neither of them survived."

He shuffles closer to me and plants a soft kiss on my forehead.

"Is that why you didn't want to go ice skating?" he asks quietly.

Embarrassment reddens my cheeks. "It's stupid, I know. The ice won't crack at an indoor ice rink."

"You don't have to explain. I get it." He offers me a reassuring smile.

I figure I may as well tell him everything. I trust him. "I was ten. My grandma, my mom's mom, brought me up in this house."

"And your grandma?"

"She passed away last year. On Christmas Eve." That's also one of the reasons I don't have a Christmas tree up. It seems wrong to celebrate now.

"Oh, Angel." He cups my face. "I'm so sorry." His response is laced with sympathy.

"It's just me now." I look around my bedroom. "And this giant house."

"It's a fucking phenomenal house."

I'm now the proud owner of a ten-bedroom mansion along the most exclusive street in all of Castleview Cove; Cherry Gardens Lane.

"This room, the living room, and the kitchen are the only rooms I've remodeled so far. There is still heaps to do," I sigh. "It's a huge job and I don't have much free time."

"There's no rush."

My attention is now firmly back on Gabe's gorgeous face. "I know. One day at a time." Reaching up, I run my hands through his wavy locks. "What about you? Where do you live?"

"You really don't know?"

I pull my brows together. "Should I?"

"Well, I know everything about everyone, and I've only lived in Castleview Cove for three weeks. People do like to gossip around here."

He's not wrong about that.

I inhale a deep breath at the realization of what he just said, flabbergasted by his news. "You live in Castleview Cove? Where? How? Why? Where did you move from?"

"I'll start with your first question." His deep laugh makes the mattress vibrate beneath us. "I do live in Castleview Cove. I live six houses down from here."

"No way," I exclaim. *How have I never seen him?*

"Way." A wide toothy smile curves his lips. "I drive into the city most days and on the other days I work from home or go out to emergency call outs for the more technical problems. I love it here, and I've always wanted to live by the sea. I've lived in Glasgow since I left university but living somewhere more serene and peaceful was so appealing. I was growing tired of city life. I didn't have a garden or garage to park my car, so I moved here. The air is fresh, the castle is beautiful, the town is magical, and then..." He pauses as if stopping himself from saying anything. "... you're here."

My heart does a cartwheel in my chest. "You didn't just move here because of me?"

He shakes his head. "No, I didn't but I was already looking at houses in the area. Then you hired my company to install your restaurant management software. It was as if fate landed at my feet. I knew you were special from the first day I met you in the doorway of Luminescence."

I rest my hand on his firm pec. "I can't believe you live here and I just thought you worked for GD Software. I didn't realize you owned it."

"GD Software... Gabriel Duncan Software."

I roll onto my back, covering my face with my hands. *How embarrassing, I didn't notice.*

Gabe climbs on top of me, pulling my hands off my flushed cheeks and pushing them up over my head.

"You have a busy brain with lots going on. You can't do and notice everything. Like I keep telling you, you need a day off and someone to take care of you, Angel."

He's right, I do.

"In two days it's Christmas. I'll rest and reset my observation skills then," I giggle.

"Until then, I'm going to take care of you." He moves down my body, nudging my thighs open as he settles between my legs. "In every way I can."

Kissing the skin across my tummy and my hips, he moves down to my pussy, parting my lower lips with his skilled fingers, exposing me to him. "You have such a beautiful pussy." He disappears between my thighs as he licks me from back to front, making me push my hips into his face. "You taste like honey. I can't get enough." Hot breath dances across my sensitive bud as he pulls back my hood, stretching me in pleasurable ways I've never experienced before.

"Relax, Angel. I'm going to make you feel so good." My body feels completely boneless as he makes me come another four times before I have to leave for my midday shift at the restaurant.

We part, reluctantly promising to see each other after Christmas, because we are unable to make our schedules work before then.

The next few days are painful. It's stupid to miss someone so much, even though I've just met them, but I do. And he seems to miss me too. We text each other relentlessly and he calls me every moment he can to check up on me and ask me how my day is.

The warmth that's taken up residence in my heart makes me feel calm and happy knowing I have someone who is interested in me, for me, and wants to do everything in his power to please me.

He's become my new addiction. I crave him and the strange flutter in my heart that keeps making an appearance, happens every time I remind myself of his words. *"I want you to be mine. I'm going to marry your fine ass and we're going to fuck every day and have lots of babies."*

For the next two days, I skip and swoon around my restaurant, thumbing my gold necklace, to feel closer to him. In a lust-filled haze, I charm diner after diner, but barely catch up on any sleep, only returning to my house to change between shifts.

I work myself into a bone deep exhaustion, using work to distract me from the one-year anniversary of my grandma's passing... and the constant longing I feel for Gabe.

When my final shift ends at midnight on Christmas Eve, I fall into my soft bed.

Happy knowing that for the next two days, I can stay in bed, finally able to rest and reset, but sad that Gabe won't be there with me to recreate our twelve-hour sex marathon.

Just two more days and I'll see him again.

I've been waiting my whole adult life to meet someone like him, so I can wait another two days.

I'm lying to myself.

I wish he was here.

CHAPTER 7

HOLLY - CHRISTMAS DAY

It's Christmas Day and just like the weatherman predicted, we have a white Christmas.

Fresh snow fell overnight, covering my garden in a white sparkly blanket.

I gaze out through the window at the backyard as I snuggle deep down into my giant, cozy bed. Surrounded by empty candy wrappers and cookie trays, I am prepared and stocked up, ready to do whatever the hell I want today.

If hunger hits me later, I will eat the food that Thomas, my head chef, wrapped up for me and is now sitting in my refrigerator. I haven't looked, knowing whatever is in there, it will be delicious.

Tucking into another bag of chips, watching *Bridget Jones' Diary*, I crack the cucumber face mask I've had on my face, for much longer than advised, when I laugh at the funny scene playing out on the screen.

I wanted Christmas Day to feel like a day off, rather than a morbid day, where it's glaringly obvious I'm all alone. I'm nailing it so far.

Although I did have the same thought last year too when I wished I had at least one sibling to share the holidays with. I mean, Christmas is supposed to be about family and gift giving. Me, I have no family to speak of and only one gift. Although it was a beautiful gift that Lucy, Alan, and Izzy bought me; a framed photo of us four on the beach this summer building sandcastles. Without them in my life, Jenna, and the restaurant, I would have lost myself completely this past year. Even though it sucks to spend Christmas on my own, I have a lot of people in my life who care about me and my staff have become my family.

The chime from my front door echoes through my empty house, startling me.

Deciding it's most likely Mrs. Everett from next door, I jump out of bed. Every year she makes fresh mince pies on Christmas morning, and every year she hand delivers them to the few houses in the street. I run down the stairs, my mouth watering at the prospect of more comfort food I can devour later.

Unlocking the door, I pull it open with haste. "Mrs. Ever—" I stop speaking instantly when I'm met with Gabe's gorgeous face and not the one I was expecting.

A slow, lazy grin forms across his lips. "What is that?" He points to my face.

My mouth drops open. "Oh, my God." I slam the door on him.

His laughter bellows out loudly as I stand in my hallway, staring at my now closed front door.

"Open up, Holly."

"No." I can't let him see me like this.

"I've seen *every* part of you, Angel. Now open the goddamn door," he coaxes me.

I bite my lip, weighing up my options.

"I'll wait here all day until you do. It'll be a shit Christmas, but I'll do it."

I roll my eyes and open the door again to find him leaning casually against the doorway.

"Merry Christmas, beautiful." He's grinning at me, his white teeth sparkling.

I play with the hem of my top. "Merry Christmas," I whisper, avoiding his gaze.

"Is that sloths on your pajamas?" He squints to get a better look. "And are they drinking coffee and hanging from pink iced donuts? Cute."

I scowl at him as he mocks me.

He points to my face again. "Beauty mask?"

I nod my head, embarrassed by my appearance.

"Is this how you're spending your Christmas Day?"

I sigh, tilting my head to the side. "That's the plan."

"How long will it take you to get out of those mighty sexy pajamas that, for your information, are giving me a hard on just looking at them, take that face mask off, shower, and throw on some clothes?"

Confused, all I can say is, "Huh?"

"How long will it take you to get showered and dressed?"

I don't know why he's asking. "About thirty minutes." Twenty, if I don't wash my hair. "Why?"

He jumps back down the doorsteps leading to my driveway, disappears round the corner, then reappears again with a fully decorated Christmas tree he's obviously been hiding.

Carrying the heavy tree as if it weighs nothing, he's back up the steps, and inside my house. Completely speechless, I follow him into my living room, watching him in shock as he positions it perfectly inside the nook of my bay window.

"Perfect." He looks at me. "Thirty minutes is enough time for me to finish decorating your tree and add the lights."

"Ehhhh..." My mouth opens and shuts like a fish out of water. "I don't... I don't have any lights."

"That's what I thought, just as well I do. They are in my car." He walks past me in a rush. "You have half an hour to change," he shouts over his shoulder. "And pack an overnight bag."

"What?" I yell, feeling like I might be having an elaborate Christmas dream.

"Get in the shower, Angel. Twenty-nine minutes left."

Bemused, through my open front door, I watch him open the driver door of his metallic red pickup truck, pull out a box, of what I presume are Christmas tree lights, and bring it back inside my house, where he peels his winter coat off.

"Twenty-eight minutes. Go." He smacks my sloth pajama covered ass as he passes, making me snap out of my stupor and stomp into my living room.

"What are you doing?" My voice now two pitches higher than normal.

He unboxes the fairy lights.

"Gabe?" I raise my voice to get his attention, cracking my facemask even more, flakes dropping to the floor like snowfall.

Twisting his head to face me, he frowns. "You can't have Christmas without a Christmas tree. It's too Grinch-like. Very uncool. I decided we're spending Christmas Day together, Angel." He checks the time on his fancy wristwatch. "Twenty-seven minutes left. And pack some snow boots."

"Gabe, what are you doing here? Should you not be with your family?" He stops fiddling with the lights, placing them on the coffee table and moves in my direction.

Standing toe to toe, he tips my chin up.

"You're spending Christmas Day with me and my family. I will not let you spend the holidays by yourself." He bops my nose.

My heart pounds hard in my chest. "I can't spend the day with people I don't know." *That sounds awful.*

"Yes, you can. They will be your family one day, too."

"You are crazy." Nervous laughter flutters in my throat. *Was he serious about knowing I'm the one that he wants to marry? Surely not.*

"Confident. There's a difference." He quirks a brow. "Now, get up those stairs, shower, and get dressed. You can get back into these pajamas if you want, but you have a drink stain on them."

How embarrassing.

He continues, "Or wear a dress, or whatever, but pack a bag and meet me down here in twenty minutes."

"You said I had twenty-seven minutes left." I slap his shoulder playfully.

"I will say anything to make you get ready quicker. I'm hungry and my mom cooks a mean Turkey. Her stuffing is the best. Now go." He turns me around to face the doorway.

Before I can move, he spanks my ass again, then pulls my hair to the side and kisses my nape. "I can't wait to kiss you again, but I'm not kissing you with what looks like the cream off a trifle all over your face." He plants another soft kiss on the space between my neck and shoulder. As if someone opened the front door, letting the unwelcome icy air in, I shiver from his touch. "You smell like cookies and candy." His warm breath heats my skin, and a shockwave of tingles runs across my body, making my nipples pebble. "It's supposed to snow again. We need to leave as soon as you're ready."

"Where are we going?" Needy hands dig into my hips as he rubs his hard length between the crack of my ass, feeling every thick inch of him through my thin cotton pajamas.

"It's a surprise." He coaxes me out of the living room, back into the hall.

Needing no further encouragement, excited that I'm getting to spend the day with him, I'm ready and sitting in the passenger seat of his truck in less than fifteen minutes.

Where are we going?

CHAPTER 8

HOLLY

We drove for only fifteen minutes, through the winding snow-covered roads, to the log cabins around Loch Castleview.

Nestled within the woods, Gabe's parent's holiday home came into view as Gabe's truck rocked from side to side down the uneven driveway.

He held my hand on the short drive here, asking me questions about my life, the things I love, from music to food, and the countries I would most like to visit. He sang along to the Christmas songs on the radio, forcing me to join in. And we laughed like we had known each other a lifetime. The man is truly one of a kind.

My heart fluttered in my chest when he pulled my hand onto his lap, threaded his fingers into mine, and then kissed my knuckles.

Everything he does makes me feel safe, completely adored, and like I belong.

Not only is Gabe a *babe*, he's smart, funny, and kind. So kind. Telling me in the truck that no one should ever have to spend Christmas Day by themselves, and promising it will never happen again.

Does he mean *we'll* be together every Christmas?

I hope so.

Helping out in the kitchen, I peel the carrots over the sink. Gabe's mom, Georgina, appears by my side. "I hope my noisy mob hasn't scared you away." She nudges my shoulder, making me laugh.

"They haven't. Not even in the slightest." I don't tell her, but I would love to be part of an incredible family like hers. They're boisterous, loud, fun, and most of all, they all love each other deeply. It's palpable.

They all need name badges, though; there're nieces and nephews, too many to count, brothers, sisters, partners, wives, and husbands. I forgot who was who after being introduced to the third sister, or was it the third brother? Who knows?

"He's never brought a girl here on Christmas Day since him and Alice split up five years ago," Georgina tells me as she turns the tap on to wash her hands.

"Alice?" I look up at Gabe's brother's fiancée who I was introduced to earlier. I remember her. It's hard not to. She's beautiful; all high cheekbones and piercing blue eyes.

"Yes, Holly. That Alice."

My shoulders become taut with tension, and I stop peeling the vegetables. *Shit, now I know why I'm here.*

"You've got nothing to worry about, Holly." She gifts me a warm smile.

Don't I?

"Will you excuse me? I need some fresh air." Dropping the peeler with a clatter against the chopping board, wiping my hands against my pencil skirt thighs, I'm out through the backdoor quicker than you can say *Merry Christmas.*

I hear Georgina calling my name, but I close the door behind me, not looking back.

Stepping into the snow-covered garden in my stupidly impractical high-heels. I don't care if I freeze my toes off. I don't want to go back inside.

Even though I'm going to have to.

How stupid am I to come here today? Expecting to fit in with people I don't know. I don't even know *him*. Well, I do, but not well enough to *know* him, know him.

"I can hear the chatter in your head from here." Gabe's deep voice cuts through my thoughts.

Turning to face him, I find him leaning against the pillar of the porch. Arms wrapped around himself; feet crossed at his ankles.

He looks like something out of GQ magazine, in his casual navy chinos and cream woolen jumper. With his thick, black-rimmed glasses firmly in place, he makes sexy geek chic look effortless.

I really like Gabe and I thought maybe, just maybe, he might have been the one.

Oh, get a grip. Holly. He only brought you here to make his ex-girlfriend jealous. Poor Holly. The little girl who grew up with no parents and now has no family to lean on, share her life or spend the holidays with.

"I don't want your pity." I sound harsher than I want to, but I don't want anyone pitying me.

"I know you don't," he says firmly.

"So, why did you bring me here?" I ask with suspicion.

Unblinking he says, "Because I wanted to."

"Did you bring me here because you felt sorry for me?"

"No," he answers me firmly.

"Did you bring me here because you wanted to make Alice jealous? Your mom said you haven't brought another woman here since her. She's marrying your brother. That must hurt. Are you still in love with her?"

He shakes his head, calmly taking his first step down the stairs of the raised porch toward me.

In only my thin silk blouse and black pencil skirt, I'm shivering as the sub temperatures wrap around me like a tight coat, chilling me to the bone. I move my hand to the gold holly necklace he gave me and twist the amulet between my fingertips.

"Holly, Alice and I dated over five years ago. We went on four dates. One of those was Christmas Day because my mom told me to invite her. We never even slept together; we both agreed there was no spark between us. The Christmas I brought her, she met my brother, and they hit it off. There is no animosity between us, no jealously, no anything."

"Right." Suddenly feeling stupid at being so presumptuous and misunderstanding his mom's words, I chew the side of my mouth nervously.

He's moved closer without me noticing and now, toe to toe, inches apart, we stand facing each other.

He continues, "I have dated on and off for the last few years, but I haven't been with anyone in over a year and never met anyone I have ever wanted to bring for Christmas dinner, or spend every day and night with, text every minute of every day, buy a Christmas tree for."

I chuckle.

"You're mistaken. It's not pity in my eyes." He cradles my face with his giant hands and I let him. "It's pure admiration at how strong you are. You are one of the most determined, strong-minded, driven women I have ever had the pleasure of being in the presence of, and I want to spend all day, every day, with you... if you'll let me."

"Forever though, right? That's the terms of spending

time with me because you're going to marry me," I jest nervously, laughter bubbling in my chest.

"Forever is right. I've never been surer of anything before." He kisses me deeply, pouring all of his desire for me through his touch.

If every day feels like this with him, I want to spend them all with him too.

It's as if all my Christmases have come at once.

Heat sizzles between us, crackling as if an electrical current is flowing through us like pure positive energy.

Two things happen at once; I feel warm and joyful— complete happiness warms my body from my nose to my toes—and for the first time in a year, I don't feel alone.

I feel completely adored as we share a kiss of all kisses. Savoring every moment, we lose ourselves in each other for what feels like forever. Wrapping my arms around his neck, we both smile in contentment against each other's lips.

"You'll spend every Christmas with me from now on, Angel."

"Okay," I agree, my giddy heart spinning in my chest.

"Are you ready for present opening time?"

My eyes widen in panic. "I didn't get you anything. I did, however, bring a very naughty selection of underwear with me, though, that I bought on Christmas Eve."

"You're my Christmas present." Entwining our fingers, he motions for us to move back inside the warmth of the log cabin.

"Are you going to unwrap me later?" My voice low and breathy.

"You can count on it. We have the private lodge down the garden all to ourselves tonight."

I can't wait.

My back to his front, I'm sitting on the floor nestled safely between Gabe's legs as we watch everyone exchange presents. His fingers have been tickling my upper arm the entire time we've sat here. He's super romantic, and he seems to like touching me, which I thoroughly enjoy.

Gabe sure has a thing for spoiling people. He bought extravagant gifts for everyone; designer handbags and earrings for his sisters and race experience days for his brothers. He even paid off his younger sister's student loans for her. He's obviously very successful and generous with his money, which makes me adore him even more.

We all laughed until our stomachs ached when his oldest brother gave his youngest brother a pair of novelty blow up boobs. Stating that it's the only boob squeeze he'll ever get again if his two years of not dating anyone continues.

Having never experienced what it's like to be part of a big family, I find myself craving to be part of this close knit one.

"I have something for you," Gabe whispers in my ear as a square-shaped, red wrapped gift magically appears in front of my eyes.

I stare at it for a beat too long. "Open it," Gabe urges me as he lays the small but heavy present on my lap.

Untying the gold bow, before carefully removing the wrapping paper, I reveal a black box.

Flipping the lid open, I pull in a breath when electric blue and green colors sparkle back at me.

"It's really heavy." My hands are shaking when I tip the box up and catch the shiny sphere in my hand.

"It's a paperweight," he whispers against the shell of my ear.

Cupping my hand around the glass ball, I hold it up. The neon blue and green tones shimmer, dazzling me under the light. "It's beautiful."

"It's Aurora Borealis."

"The Northern Lights," I reply, my voice sounding dreamy as the swirling colors mesmerize me. "It's why I chose the blue color for my restaurant. I've always wanted to go."

"I know. I read your story on your website," he murmurs in my ear as I get lost in the glistening ball of magic.

"We leave tomorrow," Gabe announces.

I twist my head to look at him and I'm met with those deep brown eyes that I want to swim into and never come out of. "What do you mean?"

"Me and you. We're going to Norway to see the real thing. We leave tomorrow for a week, and we're bringing in the New Year together," he says firmly.

Is he for real?

"I-I have a restaurant to run," I stutter.

"All sorted. Jenna is running the show for the next week."

I look back at the iridescent paperweight in wonder. "We're going here?"

"Yes, tomorrow, Holly."

A small tear trickles down my cheek. It's the most thoughtful thing anyone has ever done for me.

"Thank you," I whisper.

Gabe hooks his knuckle under my chin, lifting my face to his. "Those better be happy tears." He grins wider than the Forth Road Bridge.

I nod, unable to speak as he plants soft kisses on my lips.

"Awwwww." Everyone in the room swoons having watched our romantic moment.

Tucking myself into his shoulder in embarrassment, he wraps me in his arms. "You'll get used to this lot. Nothing is private."

"That's why you're staying in the guest lodge tonight, you two." One of his sisters pipes up, making everyone chuckle.

Oh God, world, swallow me up now.

Secretly, I relish in the fact that I may have found my place in the world, with this beautiful family.

CHAPTER 9

HOLLY

It's been the best Christmas day that I can remember since I was nine years old; the last Christmas I had together with my mom, dad, and grandma. I never knew my grandfather, nor did my mom know her own father, either. Once my grandma and him got divorced, when my mother was just a baby, she never heard from him again.

And my father's parents passed long before I was born, so I never knew them either.

Although it was just the four of us, we always had the best Christmases together and I knew I was loved deeply. I always felt safe. It always felt like home.

I forgot that feeling along the way.

Until now. With Gabe and his incredible family.

I step out of the adjoining bathroom of the lodge apartment we are staying in for the evening, hoping he likes his *present*.

"Holy fuck, Angel. What are you wearing?" He sits up, the sheet falling from him, showing me he's naked in the bed; the taut muscles of his washboard stomach ripple as he moves.

"A body bow." I bite my lip suggestively. "It's so you can unwrap me."

He curls his pointer finger, beckoning me to go to him.

On hands and knees, I crawl up the bed, bracketing my body over his.

"Merry Christmas, Gabriel," I whisper, straddling his thighs for him to get a good look at me, making him instantly hard.

"This bow barely covers a thing." He slips the thin ribbon covering my pussy to the side, then slides a thick finger deep inside of me, then another.

Moaning, I say, "I think that's the point." I rock my hips, fucking his fingers.

"You are dripping for me already." He's right. I can feel the slickness of my juices running down his fingers, hitting my thighs.

My fingernails dig into the flesh of his shoulders. "It's what you do to me."

"Only me."

"Yes." I cry when he curls his fingers against my inner walls, hitting that sweet spot deep in my core.

"You're so beautiful, Angel. Fucking beautiful when you fuck my fingers."

I whimper at his dirty talk.

"Do you want to come?" He licks his way down my neck.

"Yes." My hips pump his fingers faster. "Gabe," I moan his name.

He pulls one side of the red bow down that's barely covering my breasts, exposing my pebbled nipple, then pulls it into his mouth. Hard.

He bites, then licks it.

Having spent twelve hours with me in my bed, he now knows exactly what I like.

On the edge, about to come. He pulls his fingers out of me and I almost sob in response.

"You're not coming yet." He bites my breast and I know he's going to leave a mark. He wants to brand me as his; I want that too.

Pushing his fingers back into my body, the orgasm that was flirting with me before it makes its appearance again, and with a few more thrusts I feel myself coming.

"Stop." Gabe holds still. "Not yet."

My inner walls squeeze his fingers. "I need to... I need to come, Gabe."

"I love it when you beg, Angel." His fingers move inside of me again. "*Now* come for me." Moving faster, pushing in harder, his thumb rubs my clit and I explode around his fingers, clenching them tight as I come for him, hard. So hard, a million glowing stars dance behind my eyes in vivid greens and blues.

My body deliciously spent, I fall against him, curling into him, in awe of the power he has over me.

"Good girl," he praises me, kissing my shoulder, and I shudder at his words. His sexy bedroom mouth is a complete contrast to how he acts professionally, and I love how it's only me that gets to hear those words. No one else.

I lean out of our embrace and push him back onto the mattress.

Lifting his hand to remove his glasses, I stop him, instructing him to keep them on.

"You like them?"

"I love them."

He narrows his eyes. "Could you love me?" His face turns serious.

"I think that's the only direction for us," I say confidently, knowing just how easy it would be to fall for him, knowing deep down I already started.

He smirks, as if knowing the inevitable.

Without giving him any warning, I slide down his hard length, making him clench his eyes shut. "Fuuccckkk" he groans, digging his fingertips into the skin of my thighs.

"Look at me," I demand, feeling in control as I move leisurely up and down his huge cock.

With his eyes on me, I reposition my feet, laying them flat against the mattress in a squat position.

He shakes his head from side to side. "I won't fucking last if you bounce up and down my cock like this," he says, almost as if in pain.

"I know, but we have all night. I want you to come deep inside my pussy."

"Fucking hell," he hisses, his cock twitching inside of me. He pushes his fingertips under his glasses into his eye sockets. "Dirty talking, Angel," he mutters to himself.

I laugh. My pussy squeezing his cock in response.

"Holy shit." He grabs onto my ass.

"Ready?" I don't wait for a response as I bear down on him and back up again.

"Oh, fuck." He painfully pinches my skin, arching his neck, pushing the back of his head deep into the mattress.

Moving faster, I squat, my thigh and calf muscle already burning in this position. I squeeze my inner walls, desperate to chase my own release. His balls slap off my pussy, my clit connecting with his public bone on every downward drop onto his cock. Using his chest as leverage, I go even faster. Undulating my hips in waves, the thick head of his cock hits my G-spot in the most delicious way, and like a clap of thunder, I come again so fast I feel dizzy.

Gabe throws his hands out to the sides, balling the bedsheet into his fists. He calls out my name as I clench around him, my release coating his cock in my juices. He thrusts his hips up, then shoots his load inside of me, filling me with his cum.

He lies there panting and moaning as he comes down from his climax, his chest moving up and down as he tries to calm his breathing.

I slowly lie down on top of him, my whole body feeling like I've had a full body workout, burning off the rich Christmas dinner we ate earlier.

Wrapping me in a bear hug, he kisses the top of my head.

"Holy shit, you make me come so hard. You turn me on so fucking bad, Angel."

"You haven't fully unwrapped me yet," I mumble, rubbing the huge bow, still tied around me, against his broad chest, where his heart beats faster than a bullet train.

Still inside of me, he flips us over unexpectedly, causing me to let out a yelp at his wrestling-like movement.

"Let's unwrap you now, shall we?"

"You saved the best until last."

"You're the best present I've ever had." His voice laced with lust and want.

I think he might be mine too.

Happiness flows through me like warm honey, "Merry Christmas, Gabe."

"Merry Christmas, Holly."

CHAPTER 10

HOLLY - BOXING DAY

"I miss you." I crouch down and wipe the snow off the headstone.

Each of their names glitter back at me as the winter sun hits the gold letter against the black marble.

These three wonderful humans were the most important people in my life. They still are.

Laying the red poinsettias into the fluffy snow at the base of their headstone, I say, "I am going away for a few days, but I'll be back. Promise." I've never let a week pass without visiting them at least once.

Twisting my neck, I catch sight of Gabe leaning against his red truck, looking all sexy and suave. His eyes crinkle around the sides as he smiles softly at me.

I turn my head to look at their grave again and whisper, "I had a really nice Christmas this year. I think I'm going to be okay, guys."

Just then a fat red breasted robin lands on top of the marble. The beautiful bird sings a happy chirp before flying away again.

"You sent me Gabe, didn't you?" I double pat the stone and rise to my feet. "Thank you."

"I hate to do this, Angel, but we have a flight to catch." Gabe appears by my side.

I look at my mom, dad, and grandma's embossed names. "We're off to Norway, guys. Can you believe it?" I do a little squeal. I'm so excited.

"I'll have her back safe and in one piece, I promise." Gabe joins in my one-way conversation with my family.

Yup, I think I'm going to be just fine.

The Days Between Christmas & New Year (The Days You Have No Idea What Date or Day Of The Week It Is)

There are no words to describe how I feel as Gabe makes love to me because that's what he is doing. He's making love to me.

Blue and green, sometimes pink and purple, northern lights dance above us. Showering us in a kaleidoscope of light through the glass dome of the pod Gabe hired for the evening.

It's been the most romantic four days of my life. The silent whale watching experience, as well as a tour of the magnificent fjords, was incredible, but making love under the Aurora Borealis in this transparent bubble dome has been the highlight of the holiday.

Everything Gabe planned has been utter perfection.

Surrounded by snow in the middle of nowhere, which makes me feel like we're in our very own snow globe, Gabe thrusts in and out of my wet heat.

Cupping my face with loving hands, his eyes fill with emotion. "I'm falling for you, Angel," he breathes against my lips.

Tracing his back and shoulders with my fingertips, I drag my nails over his skin, making him moan into my mouth as he captures my lips. Our tongues twisting and turning around one another.

"Gabe," I moan, as he drives himself deeper, my legs locking around his waist. "I'm falling with you."

He rests his forehead against mine, a faint smile twisting his mouth to the side at my admission.

Leisurely rocking together, in a slow rhythmic pace, he simultaneously teases my clit with his pelvic bone, gently edging me toward my orgasm.

He slides his warm hand up my thigh, over my hip, and grabs my ass, pushing himself into me deeper.

Eyes lock, we move together as he takes his time between thrusts.

I let out a long moan when my orgasm hits, the iridescent spirals of light moving across his broad frame, lighting him up, making him look as if he's almost glowing.

As he nears his own climax, his balls slap against me as he moves faster, crying out each other's names under the stars as we come together. It's so beautiful I can barely catch my breath as the electric patterns of light bounce through the glass.

Slowly, we kiss. "I'm never letting you go," he whispers.

"I don't want you to."

I'm never letting go of him either.

New Year's Eve

"Five, four, three, two, one. Happy New Year." Cheers of celebrations go off around us as we welcome in the New Year in the beautiful Norwegian town of Tromsø.

Gabe's lips dust mine as fireworks explode in the sky, crackling, banging, and whizzing, making the sky light up in shimmering tones of gold, green, and blue.

"Happy New Year, Angel." He kisses me with the magic of his mouth, unlocking my heart and soul, and I willingly hand him them both over. They're safe with him.

Wrapped in each other's arms, in harmony with one another, we both break our kiss to look up at the spectacular display.

"So beautiful," I gasp, watching the sky fill with vibrant colors and light.

"You are," he whispers.

I drop my head to be greeted by a smiling Gabe. "You are so beautiful, Holly."

"You are like a dream come true," I admit. Our whirlwind romance has me in a spin.

"Not dreaming, Angel. This is real." His words make me feel like I'm drifting along on a big fluffy snow cloud.

His next words catch me off guard "This time next year. You'll be Mrs. Duncan." He almost crushes me in his tight embrace, my head fitting perfectly between his shoulder and neck, drinking in his spicy cologne as if it's casting me under his spell.

"You're insane." I shake my head in wonder, bathing in the confidence he displays in our connection.

"You'll see, Angel. In twelve months' time, we'll come back to this exact spot, stand in this town square at the same time, under the fairy lights and fireworks, and you'll be my wife."

An emotional ache grows in my throat and I breathe out

a simple, "Okay." Agreeing with him, how can I disagree? He's so positive and makes no attempt to hide the fact that this is what he wants.

Me.

Us.

Warm fingers curve under my chin. "You've all I've ever wanted, Holly."

My heart beats so wildly in my chest that I'm surprised he can't hear it. "You made all my Christmas dreams come true."

"I'm going to make *all* your dreams come true."

He may call me his Angel, but I know that he's mine.

My guardian angel.

My Gabe.

In this moment, as we kiss under the stars, under the dawn of a New Year, and the crackling fireworks, from now on, I'll never be alone again.

The End - Merry Christmas &
Happy New Year!

ALSO BY VH NICOLSON

The Triple Trouble Series

Hunting Eden - The Triple Trouble Series (Book 1):
mybook.to/huntingeden_VHNicolson

Inevitable Ella - The Triple Trouble Series (Book 2):
mybook.to/inevitableella_VHN

Unexpected Eva - The Triple Trouble Series (Book 3):
mybook.to/unexpectedeva

The Boys of Castleview Cove

Lincoln - The Boys of Castleview Cove (Book 1):

mybook.to/LincolnVHNicolson

Jacob - The Boys of Castleview Cove (Book 2):

mybook.to/Jacob_VHNicolson

Owen - The Boys of Castleview Cove (Book 3):

mybook.to/OwenVHNicolson

Frozen Flames (A Rekindled Ice Hockey Romance)
mybook.to/FrozenFlames_VHN

ACKNOWLEDGMENTS

I hope you loved reading Holly and Gabe's little love story as much I have loved writing it - it's a wee shortie *from* a wee shortie - I am only four foot eleven!

A massive THANK YOU to Sarah, my editor at The Word Emporium for putting up with me and not moaning at me when I made the decision, at the very last minute, to write a Christmas novella. Thank you for always being wonderful and slotting me in!

To Carolann... my enthusiastic beta reader... thank you.

To Lizzy, my beautiful alpha reader from across the pond. Thank you.

To all of the bookstagrammers, booktokers and book bloggers, a huge thank you for all of your support and the beautiful graphics and videos you create, every day you blow me away.

And to you, the spicy book reader, thank you for taking a leap of faith on a new-ish author, you have no idea how much that means to me, I am eternally grateful and without you, I wouldn't keep following my dream of becoming a full-time author. THANK YOU! Mwah x

ABOUT THE AUTHOR

Since writing her first contemporary romance novel over lockdown, Vicki is now completely smitten with writing love stories with happily ever afters. VH Nicolson was born and raised along the breathtaking coastline in North East Fife in Scotland. For more than two decades she's worked throughout the UK and abroad within the creative marketing and design industry, as a branding strategist and stylist, editor of a magazine and sub-editor of a newspaper. Married to her soul mate, they have one son. She has a weakness for buying too many quirky sparkly jumpers, eating Belgium buns, and walking the endless beaches that surround her beautiful Scottish hometown she's now moved back to.

Website: vhnicolsonauthor.com
Facebook Group:
bit.ly/VHNicolsonFacebookReaderGroup

Printed in Great Britain
by Amazon